The Book of
ELLIE

By Jocelynn Mitchell

Illustrated by Alicia Mitchell

Published and printed in the USA.

ISBN: 9798359427180

Dedicated to all the awesome dogs out there
who make their owners' lives amazing!
-Ellie

P.S. Don't forget to follow me on
TikTok and Instagram so you won't
miss my next book and updates of my life.

I'm Ellie, and before anyone else has a chance to slander my good name, I want you to know....

I'm the
BEST
WORST DOG EVER!!!!

My owners **adore** me!
I mean, can you blame them???

I'm the best at so many things, but I am the
ABSOLUTE BESTEST at:

-**Coming**

-**Staying**

-**Racing**

-**Snuggling**

-**Begging**

-**Pooping**

-**Guarding**

and... -**Sleeping**

I'm also **the cutest!**

Coming

I know exactly what 'come' means.....

'Come' means
"Stay where you are."

OR

"Walk further away."

It can also mean...

"RUN AS FAST AS YOU CAN IN THE OTHER DIRECTION!!!"

Staying

'Stay' means **1 of 2 things:**

   1. If you are in the house, 'stay' means sneak up on your owner like a ninja and trip them... **HARD!**

   2. If you somehow find yourself outside (whether on a leash or by sneaking through an open door) and your owner tells you to stay, that means **"Run into oncoming traffic!"**

Snuggling

Snuggling is when
you wait for your owner to fall
asleep in their favorite chair.

Then...

JUMP, ATTACK, BITE, and SCRATCH,

until they cry out with joy!

Begging

Any self-respecting dog has to know the **'Art of the Beg'.**

Step 1: Enlarge eyes to 5 times their normal size.

Step 2: Make fake tears. This enhances the large eye effect.

Step 3: Suck in your stomach, so that it looks like you haven't eaten in days.

Step 4: Intensely stare at your owner until acknowledged. (Bark or whine if needed.)

Step 5: If all else fails...............
jump up, steal the food and **RUN!!!**

Pooping

or as I like to think of it:

Creating Masterpieces Out of Organic Matter

Only the most awesome, bestest, coolest, and smartest dogs can turn the common walk into an artistic extravaganza!

Every artist has a canvas.

Mine is grass!

But, it can't be just any old grass.

It has to be the greenest, softest, and smelliest patch on the block.

Remember, patience is key, and true art is about the journey as much as the destination.

Do not bestow your gift upon the world until you have sniffed the entire area 4,833 times and turned 175 circles, and **then....**

When you are finished, if it is truly a great piece, your owner will collect that day's masterpiece in a bag and take it home.

Guarding

If you haven't already figured it out, I live on the streets... the mean streets of the suburbs!

Danger lurks around every corner, and there are likley suspicious people and dogs that could pose a threat.

You should **ALWAYS** be on the lookout and bark loudly when someone who is up to no good walks nearby.

Yeah, you better keep walking...

Your owners will appreciate you letting them know **EVERY** time there is an intruder in the neighborhood.

Racing

When your owners are walking up or down the stairs, that means they want to race.

So make sure you **run as fast as you can** in front of them...and cut them off so they don't win!

If they happen to fall, well that's life in the fast lane.

Sleeping

There's only one way to sleep:

Wedge yourself in bed between your owners and stretch out as far and wide as you can.

If they fall out of bed...**MORE SPACE FOR YOU!**

Owners also love it when their dogs snore loudly; Imagine your nose is a speaker!

Well.... I hope you've enjoyed this book as much as I have, but I feel another **masterpiece** coming on...

 Bye!

Oh, I almost forgot....

Words, Wisdom and Pooping Schedules to Live By:

 Rule #1 is, **I'm #1!**
(Never forget, I'm the greatest!)

 Rule #2: Being told 'no' means **'Try harder!'**

 Rule #3: You don't have to be a good dog if you're cute! If not, well, **SORRY!**

 Rule #4: I never concern myself with anything **B.E.** (**B**efore **E**llie).

 Rule #5: Don't just rely on your food bowl or scraps at the table. **Anything** on the floor is fair game to eat. Just swallow it before your owner's can fish it out of your mouth!

 Rule #6: The thing about pooping schedules is, don't have one! Your owners will appreciate staying active at any time of the day!

 Rule #7: I'm the only dog my owners will **EVER** love...

The Real Ellie

This book was based on true events! Although Ellie gets herself into trouble sometimes, we could not be more proud to have her in our family. She is three years old and loves to be outside and bark at people walking by.

Made in the USA
Las Vegas, NV
10 December 2022

61646141R00017